MONSTER AND Frog

And The

ALL-IN-TOGETHER CAKE

For Grace
R.I.

For my sister
R.A.

Consultant: Prue Goodwin,
Lecturer in literacy and children's books,
University of Reading

ORCHARD BOOKS
338 Euston Road, London NW1 3BH
Orchard Books Australia
Hachette Children's Books
Level 17/207 Kent Street, Sydney NSW 2000

First published in Great Britain in 2006
First paperback publication 2007

Text © Rose Impey 2006
Illustrations © Russell Ayto 2006

A CIP catalogue record for this book is available from the British Library

ISBN 1 84121 546 5 (hardback)
ISBN 1 84362 233 5 (paperback)

1 3 5 7 9 10 8 6 4 2

Printed in China

MONSTER AND Frog

And The
ALL-IN-TOGETHER CAKE

ROSE IMPEY  RUSSELL AYTO

ORCHARD BOOKS

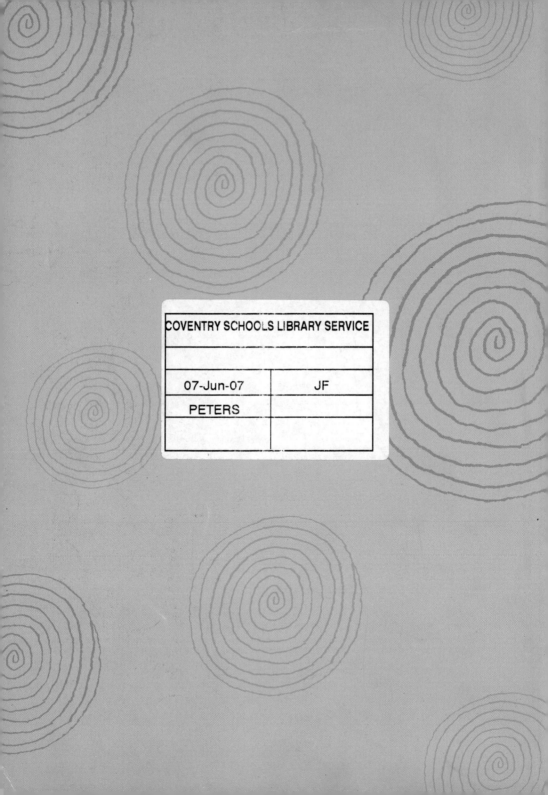

Monster has invited his sister
and her baby to tea.
He wants to make them a cake.

But Monster has never made
a cake before.

"Leave it to me," says Frog.
"I could make a cake standing
on my head."

Monster does not like the sound
of that.

Frog finds a recipe:
All-in-Together Cake - the easiest
cake in the world.

Monster does like the sound
of that.

First, says the recipe, weigh the
butter and the sugar.

Next, says the recipe, break four
eggs and add to the bowl.

"Watch this," says Frog.
"I am an expert at breaking eggs."

Frog holds an egg in each hand.
He cracks them on the side of
the bowl. But he misses.

Frog tries two more eggs.
But he misses again.

"Oh dear," says Monster.

"Breaking eggs is not as easy
as it looks," says Frog.

Next, says the recipe, weigh
the flour, then sieve it.

"This is the secret of a light cake," says Frog. "This cake will be so light it will float."

Float!

Monster does not like the sound of a floating cake.

Frog sieves the flour. It flies everywhere. Now it looks as if it is snowing.

Monster can hardly see across the kitchen.

Monster and Frog look like two snowmen.

"Look at me," says Monster.
"And look at my kitchen."

"Do not worry about that," says
Frog. "We will clear it up later."

At last everything is in the bowl.
Now, says the recipe, stir
it all together.

Monster has a big spoon ready.
He wants to stir the cake.
But Frog says, "Leave this to me.
I am an expert at stirring."

Frog stirs the cake mixture.
He stirs it faster . . .

and faster . . .

and faster.

The mixture flies all over
the kitchen.
"Stop! Stop now!" cries Monster.

Monster looks round his kitchen.
"What a mess," he says.
"Do not worry," says Frog. "I am
good at clearing up."

Now, says the recipe, put the
mixture in a cake tin.

But there is not much mixture left.
It only just covers the bottom
of the tin.

"This will be a very small cake," says Monster.

"It will rise in the oven," says Frog. "Trust me. I know all about All-in-Together Cakes."

While the cake is baking, Monster
starts to clear up.
Frog says he will help.

Mmm, delicious!

Frog is very good at clearing up!

When the cake is baked, it does not look like the lightest cake in the world.

It looks more like a pancake.

"Oh dear! Now what will I give my sister and her baby to eat?" says Monster.

Frog says he will think of something. He is full of good ideas.

Just then Monster's sister arrives.
She has a surprise for Monster.

"It is my special All-in-Together
Cake," she says.

"Mmm," says Frog, "We know all about All-in-Together Cakes, don't we, Monster?"

"We know all about eating them," says Monster. Yum yum!

MONSTER AND Frog

ROSE IMPEY 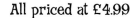 RUSSELL AYTO

Enjoy all these adventures with Monster and Frog!

All priced at £4.99

Orchard Colour Crunchies are available from all good bookshops, or can be ordered
direct from the publisher: Orchard Books, PO BOX 29, Douglas IM99 1BQ
Credit card orders please telephone 01624 836000
or fax 01624 837033 or visit our Internet site: www.wattspub.co.uk
or e-mail: bookshop@enterprise.net for details.

To order please quote title, author and ISBN
and your full name and address.
Cheques and postal orders should be made payable to 'Bookpost plc.'
Postage and packing is FREE within the UK
(overseas customers should add £1.00 per book).

Prices and availability are subject to change.